T0129017

TAKING BACK THE UNIVERSE
The Urban Sci-Fi Thriller

Trina Renee'

authorHOUSE®

AuthorHouse™
1663 Liberty Drive
Bloomington, IN 47403
www.authorhouse.com
Phone: 1-800-839-8640

Cover Artist: Giovanni Ribo

First published by AuthorHouse 8/30/2011

ISBN: 978-1-4634-4167-8 (sc)
ISBN: 978-1-4634-4168-5 (e)

Library of Congress Control Number: 2011914113

Printed in the United States of America

Any people depicted in stock imagery provided by Thinkstock are models, and such images are being used for illustrative purposes only. Certain stock imagery © Thinkstock.

This book is printed on acid-free paper.

CONTENTS

Chapter 1

IN THA BEGINNIN

"WASSUP BLOOD, YOU READY?" I asked my nigga D as I passed him tha grapes.

"Let's get this money," he said as he hit tha blunt and tucked his pistol.

We got out the car and walked over to an abandoned warehouse on 85th Ave. They was already there: our connect Antonio and some random ass nigga.

"Ay where Carlos, who dis nigga?" I demanded. "You know we don't bring in nobody else to this."

"Relax," Antonio said all calm and shit. "No need to go there blood, Carlos couldn't make it, this my cousin Rico."

"Whateva mufucka, you a cop?" D asked straight up.

"Of course not man he's good, you know me." Antonio explained.

"Exactly, but I don't know this nigga," D said. "Lift up yo shirt, you betta not be wearin a wire or it's a wrap fa yo ass."

"I ain't liftin up shit, Antonio what the fuck?" Rico asked. "I didn't come here fo this shit, you got the fuckin money or what?"

"We ain't talkin bout shit, til you lift up yo fuckin shirt, you think I'm stupid or somethin?" I shouted. "You got me hella fucked up. Unless you want this shit to get real fuckin ugly, you betta do it."

Me and D pulled out our guns and cocked em, but so did they.

"What's it gon be?' D asked.

I don't know who shot first, but I know I emptied my whole clip on them niggas.

"D you straight? We gotta cut," I yelled as I stared at they bodies on the ground. "D?"

When I didn't hear shit back, I was already knowin what I was finna see when I turned around. His chest was hella bloody and he was laid out on the concrete.

"Oh shit! I got you cousin," I screamed.

"You gon make it blood, I just gotta get you in the car."

I put him in the whip, grabbed the duffel bags and pistols and smashed outta there like Mario Andretti.

"I know exactly where to go man, you straight, we close too," I said as I looked over at him. "You just gotta stay wit me bruh."

"Donte'," he whispered.

"We almost there man, stay wit me," I pleaded.

"Te' I can feel it blood," he said hella slow. "I'm on my way."

"No don't say that, you good. I'm pullin up right now."

I ran around the car and opened the

door. He just laid there not breathin. I grabbed him and took him to my patna Jake, the only white boy I could trust to fix this shit.

"Jake," I screamed. "Davion got shot and he ain't breathin you gotta help me blood."

"Oh shit! Donte' what the fuck happened?" Jake yelled as he took it all in. "Come on D you can do it. Fuck! I gotta get these bullets out and get him stabilized."

I just stared in a daze. Jake sounded like he was miles away, like an echo. D's body just laid there, lifeless.

"Oh no stay with me!," Jake yelled.

Flat line.

Do you really wanna know my story? It ain't yo typical shit and it definitely ain't for the scary. Well sit back, cause it's gon take a minute. I been through so much crazy shit in my life that got me to where I'm at today. Everythang that happened to me made me know what I know now. I ain't gon lie to you, I definitely came a long way. I'ma take you back to tha beginnin.

Aight growin up in the hood, we was strugglin straight up. We ain't have shit. My moms been a dope fien since I was 9. My dad got killed cause of some hatin ass niggas didn't wanna see him shine when I was 8. So we was just tryina survive. Out here in Oakland, California it look nice, wit tha good weather, palm trees and shit but it really ain't. You can get murked out here for nothin. We had to do what we had to do ta make it.

That's why me and D started slangin. You was just neva finna see me up at Mickey D's flippin burgers fa pennies. Shit I had to hold down the house, I needed real dough. And befo you know it, we had a lil click poppin off. Time went on and we kept movin up. The block was crackin.

I love it out here in the Bay cause hella different races out here. And you know I'm finna take advantage. So my Mexican patnas gave me a perfect connect that got me 13 for a key. Beautiful. I took that and doubled up and doubled up. So I just been doublin eva since.

Cops a fuckin trip though. Always wanna cut. And it's never enough. They always want more and more. Fuck em. But shit, that's the game. And this shit don't never stop. Believe that shit. Niggas kill sellin it and niggas die smokin it.

I gotta whole other gold mine hustle too. I made a team full of stallion ho bitches that live on tha track fa me. A true town nigga gon always keep it pimpin feel me? International Blvd, which was originally E 1-4 and gon always be E 1-4 ta me, is tha international headquartas fa pimpin. So I was bread fa this shit. It's gon always be nothin ona bitch. All a bitch can do for me is bring me my money ya dig? Fuck a pretty bitch wit her hand out. A bitch gotta contribute. Add to the plate, fuck a date.

So as you can see, I'm busy...

But I'ma be honest wit you. I do gotta chick that hold me down you know? When I need ta get away, I go holla at her. But I ain't neva got no time. So we'll see where that go. She always wanna talk about what happened to me when I was little and my feelins and shit. And a nigga like me don't like dwellin on times when I was broke.

I'm just out here doin me. It's a dirty game and at this point, I've seen so much shit pop off, I just don't give a fuck about nobody else. People do some crazy shit out here ta get tha dough. That's how this shit really is blood. Every man fo himself...

But now everthang fuckin changed. I don't know what happened. It was lika blur or somethin. The wake. The funeral. I mean I felt like time didn't even move. I just cain't believe my patna's gone. This shit ain't right man. D was a down ass nigga blood. Man on mommas he was a loyal ass nigga. And what's so fucked up is that the niggas who did it already dead too. Cain't get revenge on nobody. Nobody to blame but myself. I think about it every fuckin second. I just keep rewindin it over and over in my head. What if I didn't say shit to Antonio, maybe he would still be here.

"You sure you don't want me to make the runs?" Scoobie asked me.

"Naw I'm good. I gotta get my mind off this shit man. I cain't stay couped up in this house no more."

"Aight, well just hit me if you need me," he said, then cut.

So I finally crawled outta bed, got dressed and walked to my garage. I usually smashed in one of my scrapers for this kinda shit, you know, just to be on the low. But none of my buckets workin, so they in the shop. So I took the next car up on tha list, my 64 mustang. But you know me, I always gotta keep my shit fresha than the next niggas. It got peanut butter candy paint, witta hemi, sittin on dubs and you know I keep em clean – Ha ha! So I put my shit in the trunk, in the double 07 compartment and dipped out.

I decided to go to the conasto on 13th Ave and Mac Arthur to get some swishers and Hen, you know, breakfast of champions.

"Aight let me hit this cona right quick." I gotta see my patna about gettin anotha connect.

Outta fuckin nowhere, 5-0 jumped behind me.

"Blurp, blurp," I instantly heard from the cop sirens.

"Fuck!," I screamed as I hit the clutch and gas. I dipped, dodged, bobbed and weaved through the traffic. I looked through the rear view mirror, and I saw like 5 fuckin cops hit every cona wit me!

"I knew I had hands with my whip, but damn! The only way you finna catch me is in a body bag BIOTCH!" I screamed out the window.

I smashed down 14th Ave., doin lika buck 50. Then outta nowhere, a blue fucked up ass Honda Civic jumped in front of me.

"Oh shit!" I screamed as I swerved out of control and flipped 3, 4 times in the air onto the side of the street.

Chapter 2

THA PIN

"DONTE'," THE WOMAN WHISPERED. "DONTE', do you hear me?"

I woke up in a hospital room handcuffed to a bed. And a nigga never wanna be in cuffs, even if a fine ass woman put you in em. I moved, sharp pains hit me from everywhere.

A white lady in a nurse's outfit looked at me with a clipboard.

"Where am I?" I asked.

"San Quinton," she explained.

"Damn, how long I been sleep?"

"3 months. You were pretty banged up when you first got here. Most people don't make it from a crash like the one you had. But you are definitely a survivor," she said as she touched my face.

"Damn, 3 months," I said. "All I remember is tryin ta shake 5-0. I guess I didn't get away huh?"

We both laughed.

"Ouch."

"Yeah looks like you'll be in here a little while longer and then sentencing."

"Great."

* * * * *

Before all this shit happened everything was gravy: cash, cars, bitches, bottles, purple and pills. Me and D was yo neighborhood Dope boys from tha Town, just doin our jobs. Playin the hand we was dealt. But like the OGs always told me, "Everythang gotta a time limit young blood. Get what you can, then split. Cause when you livin that trife-life, yo clock can stop any minute. Prison if you lucky or dead if you lucky, dependin on how you look at it." And we wasn't no fuckin different. My best patna gets murked and now I gotta do 5 years for possession and some mo shit. Damn!

Ain't like I ain't never been in the pin befo, but not for this long and neva like this. But that's the game. Shit I coulda got life fo them bodies! So I'm good. I just need to be easy and count the days til I get out.

✽ ✽ ✽ ✽ ✽

"Ay shit face, you gotta a visitor," the bitch made guard said to me.

When I walked into the visitin room, Scoobie was sittin behind the glass lookin hella shook.

"Wassup blood, how you doin in here cuzzo?" he asked all jumpy and shit.

"I'm maintainin as best I can in here," I said. "You know them mufuckas gave me 5 racks."

"I heard. Well you know I'ma hold you down while you in here blood just like you did me."

"Preciate it," I said as 5 years sank in all over again. "So what's been poppin?" I asked as I tried to get it outta my head.

"You know, niggas kinda hurtin."

And I know what he wanted to say. Since I murked the connect, streets been dryin up and they been beefin wit them Mexicans eva since.

"I know ya'll work it out," I said. "Call Tee-Tee."

"Aight, that'll work," he said. "Well I'ma cut and get shit straight. I got you on yo books so you good right?"

"Fa show."

"Well I'ma get at you later blood. Stay up."

"Peace."

* * * * *

Prison life ain't nothin no nigga eva wanna get used to. But when you in, you ain't got no choice. I hate this shit. I been here too many times befo. And fa some dumb ass reason I really fuckin thought I wasn't gone be here again. Fuck!

"What the fuck *is* this?" I grumbled to myself as I inspected the powdered shit on my plate they called food.

"Ay blood, you gon eat that?," a guy asked next to me who looked at the slop with drool in his mouth.

"Hell naw I ain't eatin that shit."

"Well can I have it?"

"Whateva man, I'm goin back to my cell."

"Good lookin out blood," he said as he started to scarf it down.

As I walked back I saw two manly ass lookin niggas layed on top of each other like it was nothin. Man I gotta get the hell outta here.

"What you in for young blood?" my cellmate asked.

And here this nigga go. I cain't stand when niggas wanna know yo personal business. Wanna be all up in yo shit. I don't know this nigga.

All I know is his name is Elder Jackson and that's what everybody called him, even the guards, which really fucked my head up of course, cause you know they don't respect nobody.

"Bein stupid," I hated to admit. "I got caught."

"Ouch," he whispered. "Well... at least you're in here for something you actually did."

"What YOU in fo?" I asked to throw the question back at him.

"Long story, but I'm sure you heard some of it," he smirked.

I heard some niggas sayin that he was a political prisoner from the Civil Rights Movement who was doin time for some shit he didn't do.

"Yeah, but I learned a long time ago to get the facts from the source."

"Wise words from such a young man," he said as he looked at me. "Well to understand, I gotta give you some background info.

See I come from a time when it wasn't all about materialism like how your generation grew up. We grew up with a real sense of community. You want the story?"

"Ain't like we got somethin else to do," I said.

"Well the Black man and woman were tired of being oppressed and having the white man's boot on our necks. I mean it was a lot different than it is now because racism and discrimination were just so much more *obvious and in your face* back then. People were getting lynched and murdered all the time just because they were Black. And we slowly realized that the only way we could really protect ourselves was to unite because there's strength in numbers. It has a greater impact to actually make a change.

"I remember what happened when Emmett Till got murdered because he supposedly whistled at a white girl. His mom had an opened casket so the world could see just how evil and demonic white people could be to us Black folks. I remember looking at the pictures in the Jet Magazine and they literally gave me nightmares.

"By the time I was in high school, my friends and I were routinely harassed by the cops for doing nothing and I really saw how the Black man could never catch a break in the white man's world. So I joined the Black Panther Party in Oakland and we helped people stop hustlin and robbin on the streets, we helped feed the children and we ran for political offices.

"Now that I look back at it all though, it was only inevitable that the system devised a way to snuff us all out because we were doing too much good," he sighed.

"So what exactly do they have you in here for?" I wondered.

"They put a cop murder rap on me," he said looking at me dead in my eyes straight to my soul. "I've been fighting it for 15,330 days." He sighed. And a few minutes passed. "But when I get to talk to young cats like you, I understand that this is all apart of God's Divine Plan because there are no coincidences in life, you remember that young blood."

"No coincidences huh?," I laughed. "Humph, so you sayin there's a reason why I'm in here now? Shiit."

"That moment of clarity will come to you young grasshopper and when it does, BOOM!," and his hands spread wide as his eyes, "You're forever changed. Here," he leaned over and passed me a worn out book.

"Slavery: The African American Psychic Trauma by Sulton and Naimah Latif. What would you do if you found out there was a major conspiracy to hide your true identity?" I read the rest of the back cover to myself.

"You can have it," he said. "It's one of my favorites. Read it and then you can come to my discussion group. We talk about everything affecting the Black Community. It'll give you some real insight on your world-view."

"Aight," I said as I looked at the table of contents. "I'm hella bored and I ain't doin nothin else in here but rottin anyway, might as well learn somethin."

✳ ✳ ✳ ✳ ✳

I don't wanna sound lame or nothin, but I really did learn somethin. I mean like my ignorance was replaced with new layers of knowledge. I know ya'll like, "Here this nigga go on that Black power shit just like every other nigga who went to tha pin." But it's somethin about time and a book that will just change you.

In a few months I read more books than I've ever read in my whole life. A fact that is sad but so true. And I seriously became a sponge for knowledge. I felt so *powerful* and I *felt* my brain grow stronger. I read: Nile Valley Contributions to Civilization, Blacked Out Through Whitewash, The Autobiography of Malcolm X, The Husia, Breaking the Chains of Psychological

Slavery, The Mis-Education of the Negro and so many others.

I even picked up a couple of grammar books and I'm getting better. Nobody put me onto the meaning of a subject-verb agreement until I got to prison. I can apply it when I feel like it instead of being held back by my ignorance.

But to be honest, English wasn't my people's original language anyway. I read a book called Talkin and Testifyin The Language of Black America by Geneva Smitherman that breaks down how Black English is a combination of English and our African languages. And since I know that, I'm not ashamed of how I talk anymore. I learned more things about the world and my people that were never even thought of in my hood.

I mean I'm still me, but I've evolved to be a better man. I know there's more to life than gettin money and gettin over. I mean that's why I'm in here in the first place because of that fucked up attitude. That's why D's gone. But I know now there is a better way.

Cause doin time, all you got is time to think about the things that lead you to the pin. What if I let Scoobie make the drop offs? What if I wasn't so fuckin stupid takin that flashy ass Stang? What if I didn't go to the conasto? That shit can drive you crazy cause any answer you give doesn't matter cause you didn't choose that one.

I've realized that I had to go through a crazy fucked up life just to wake up and realize this is a cold ass set up they got goin on here. I never really had a shot. Moms a dope fien and Pops dead and gone. We was starvin. What else was I gonna do?

Maybe I'm just a late bloomer. Shit I'm only 21. But I *feel* so must older. It feels almost like I've been here been here before. It sounds crazy I know.

Reading and studying African History, which is really human history and evolution as a whole, I found that there is only good and evil when it comes to this chess game we call life. I played on the other side long enough man. I know where that road goes like Trinity said in the Matrix and I know that definitely ain't where I wanna be.

Anthony T. Browder's book, Survival Strategies for Africans in America, says that America was conceived in sin because racism and white supremacy are the real parents, not liberty and justice. African

Americans are the step kids. When I read that I was like damn, there it is in plain English. And if we don't really study that and take it seriously, we'll never realize our *real* problems.

Livin foul just ain't the way. You see where it gets you: in here or inna box buried 6 feet deep. When I think back, I realize that I knew where I was headed, I just didn't giva fuck I guess. Or maybe I thought it wasn't gon be me. Like I was different or somethin. Back then I just lived in the moment. But now that's got me livin 2,628,000 moments in the pin. I know now that what I was really doin was tearin down myself and my community.

It's crazy tryina become a betta man when

you surrounded by psycho ass niggas. Just gotta keep my sanity. I gotta find peace somehow in this madness. I really gotta work on my concentration. Find my center.

I was just reading a book about the chakras, which are the seven centers of spiritual power in the human body: The Crown, The Third Eye, The Throat, The Heart, The Solar Plexus, The Sacral and The Base. This made me really open my eyes to how much control I could potentially have over myself if I focused. And prison is pretty much the perfect place to practice. Cause if I could make it in here, shiit, I could make it anywhere.

So I focused all my energy on not bein phased by anything. Not havin a care in the world on the inside while still maintainin my respect on the outside. Cause I'm still surrounded by crazyness nonstop.

I've learned to control myself using meditation. Everyday, for hours each day. I focus my mind on other parts of the world. Places I've never been to physically, but have been mentally. Each day I am able to go further and further away. I started with location. I studied everything I possibly could. Then I went on to sounds, smells and the temperature of the place.

That's why when me and the brothas walked in a room, there was a protective shield around us or somethin. Niggas knew that we were on somethin different. Mind elevation. So everybody always asked for Elder Jackson to speak. Everybody. It's just somethin about his words that make you get what's *really* goin on.

"I know it's hard," Elder Jackson said in low tone.

"Yeah," some people who surrounded us said.

"But we gotta hold on," he continued. "We can't give up. We gotta stay strong. We've got to do it for our ourselves. And for those who are blessed to have them, we gotta do it for our families. Now I don't know why you're in here. And to be honest, I don't care because guess what? You're here. No matter how many I wish I wouldas and couldas, you still gotta overcome what you did and adapt without it breakin ya. You gotta know that you came a long way from the stupid kid that they first put in here. You're not the same fool you used to be.

"That's why you gotta study man. Pray, read, meditate. That's the way to enlightenment. Read books of scholars like J. A. Rogers, John Henrik Clarke, Cheikh Anta Diop.

"Shit I been in here for 42 looong years man and I ain't gonna let em break me! I'm God's child! They didn't make me so how can they break me? Ya dig my brotha? You gotta know who you are man. Cause if you don't you gon start believin what they tell you. 'You ain't shit. You a heathen. Nigger. Monkey. Coon.' Everythang but a man of God.

"Do you know who you are my brotha? Or are you livin the lie you were born into? Are you still wearing mental chains of self hate for what our ancestors went through? Being sold into slavery for over 400 years. For what our grandparents went through? Dealing with living in America with their captors after they were freed. The lychings, rapings and the burning down of our towns. Or what about what we still go through? Racism, discrimination, poverty, crime and drugs in our community. Shit this vicious cycle is really why we're in here *right now*."

"What do we do?," somebody asked.

"Break the cycle within yourself. Take responsibility for your actions. Know that there is an action and a reaction in life. Either you plant good seeds or bad. Do you follow what I'm sayin to ya?"

"Yeah I do," the guy said.

"I'm gonna give you a book list to start you on the journey to change. And I will partner you up with somebody from our group to discuss what you're reading one on one."

"I'll help out," I said. "These books really

opened my eyes to a whole new world I never thought about before and to see somebody else go through that is like me doin it all over again."

Even though hella crazy shit pops off in prison, like evil racist ass guards; niggas gettin beat up, shanked, murked and raped; and nasty ass food that basically makes me throw up every time I look at it, I find peace in our study group.

I know what ya'll thinkin, "Who is this nigga?" But check it. I'm the same nigga, but I'm wiser now. I didn't have a choice really. You can get caught up in the daily bullshit of bein in here, go crazy for bein in here or try to grow from bein in here. And I ain't neva been a dumb nigga so of course

I chose the last one. I realized that I needed to analyze exactly what got me to this point in my life so maybe I could help the next young nigga not make the same choice.

For example, did you know that the word nigga was used by our ancestors before our slave masters made it derogatory? The Africans of Asia used it first. They were called the Nāgas, the divine northern gods of Buddhism. The Nāga was also represented by a snake, which symbolized divinity to the ancients because a snake has the ability to change its skin and appear to live forever. That's why we use the word so freely and don't know why. It used to bother me before sometimes to use the word, but it all makes sense now. We were somebody before our ancestors were enslaved and this is just another example of it.

"So we all just finished reading this

very powerful book, Blacked Out Through Whitewash and I know everybody has a comment so let's get started," Elder Jackson said to the group of black men seated in a circle. "Who wants to go first?"

"I guess I'll start," Michael Christianson said. "Wow is definitely a good word to use."

Mike is a cat who looked like he really don't belong here. I mean none of us do, but he looked *too* square, like he came from the burbs witta momma and a daddy who got good ass jobs and shit. And just like the rest of us, he still ends up in here. I guess it doesn't matter where you from.

"When I first read the warning that you have the right to remain ignorant and bamboozled, I was like they have started on the right foot," he said as he adjusted his glasses. "All of my life I have been raised to believe that white was always right. But little did I know they were stealing our ancestor's legacy and just wrote them right out of history. This book definitely gives so much evidence to that so you can use it in your arsenal of knowledge to fight back. Cause you guys know we're in an all out war."

"You're too right about that," Elder Jackson said. "We are in a war more than we really think about. This has been going on for thousands of years. And we are only reaping our lifetime's share of it. Our people have been dealing with this for far too long. We must fight back as best we can and unite each other.

"We need to realize that our ancestors lived righteously. And righteousness is the path to enlightenment. Ya see, slavery through the world off track. Nobody ever suffered any kind of consequence whatsoever for what happened during slavery. And because of that, their descendants have been reeking havoc on the planet ever since. SO we *must* strategize," he said as everyone clapped in agreement. "Let's continue, Donte' what did you think about the book?"

"Man um this book was eye openin for real, " I said as I took a deep breath. "I wish somebody woulda told my ass befo I started slangin packs. I just feel so dumb now doin time and shit. But at least now I know. I ain't makin no excuses fa what I did. We just didn't know no other way."

"And I was just sittin here thinkin bout everything. The shit that happened in my life that got me in here and how ya'll got in here too. This shit is soo fucked up man. I mean we all sittin here, in prison for different shit, readin these books that explain like word for word how America was built off our people and how it's made for us to go straight to the pin. And we got other books that show us what our people were doin befo we were slaves. And we weren't all in mud huts and shit like they said we were. I mean they'll have you believing that the Egyptians were White when Egypt's in hot ass Africa! That's why they don't use the land's original name Kemet. They rewrite and take everything.

"Hold on, where is it? Yeah right here in this book, um Black people were the first to create reading, writing, math, science, architecture, religion. I mean that sounds like paradise to me. Now that's a civilization. I mean that's even where Christianity and Islam came from. They don't teach you that in school. They keep those lies goin so that you will stay in their viscous cycle. It makes us not even interested in school cause what they teachin don't help us at all.

"I mean we were really the first people on this planet man. That really blows my mind. All races came from Black people and because of pangea, the planet split up and humans had to adapt to the different climates over thousands of years. But now everything is different. And slavery is the reason. This shit is crazy. It's going to take forever to get back where we used to be before that happened. I mean we don't even really know about our history before slavery.

"In the Town readin a book is like, 'Nigga you tryina be white. What the fuck you readin a book fo? Ain't nothin in that mufucka that's finna put dough in yo pocket.' Little do we know that knowledge about who we really are as a people is bigger than money, laws, I mean it's bigger than *all of this*."

"Exactly, the whole fabric of western civilization is saturated in the thievery of African culture," Sean Davis said, who was sittin next to me in the circle. "Slavery and the propaganda machine changed the game man. That's how we got to this place in our history. They enslaved our people and wrote us out of history. That's where the birth of western society comes from. Everything is upside down. Now it's like you said with that chess game we call life, it's our move. But how do we bounce back from that?"

"Unity and knowledge of self," Elder Jackson said. "Those must be our contributions, our footprints, our legacies.

We must stay strong and not forget our past because without it, we have no future. Let's take the examples our ancestors left us and use them in the present. Because patience is the greatest virtue."

"Exactly," I said as I looked into space. Somethin just clicked in my head. "Use them in the present. We need real independence. It's like we livin in the hood and only rentin, and that's why it's so fucked up. We need to our own land, but the righteous way. We haven't had it for hundreds of years. We don't know what it's like to really be free."

"So we will adjourn until next week," Elder Jackson said.

Everyone began to get up and talk to each other in small groups.

"I've got a job for you," Elder Jackson said as he walked toward me. "You would be just perfect talking to the disadvantaged youth who come here once a month."

"Why not," I said. "That's probably the least I could do considerin all the dirt I did on them streets."

"Good, well a group of 20 young men will be here next week and I really want you to tell them your story," he said. "It's very powerful."

"Fa sho," I said. "I'ma keep it all the way one hunnid too. Cause that's what they need. Somebody to keep it real and not sugar coat nothin or they gon end up in here wit us."

As I walked back to my cell I started to think about exactly what I wanted to tell these kids. Somebody had to keep it real. Cause for some reason bein gangsta is what's hot in the hood, but it seems like nobody is really breakin down the consequences to these youngstas. I really wish somebody woulda schooled me. Who knows who I woulda been.

"I see myself in every single one of ya'll," I said to the youngins. "Cause ya'll lookin at me like you don't wanna be here and that you already know everything, but if that was really the case, none of ya'll would be here right?"

"Right," they all said in a low groan.

"Let me school ya'll befo you end up in here wit the rest of us. So what did you do to end up in this program," I asked one of the kids in the group.

"Well... I was caught witta burner," he said.

"Well be happy it ain't have a body on it," I said. "How old are you?"

"13," he said.

"I would ask what the hell you doin witta burner at 13, but shit I had one at 11. But you see where that got me right? I'm up in here for being on the wrong path. And I know yall thinkin that ain't finna be me, but trust me, every single nigga in here said the same exact shit and they sittin in here wit me or they're dead. Feel me?"

Chapter 3

GOING BACK WITH ELDER JACK

I WAS BORN PAUL RICHARD Jackson on November 17, 1949 in Oakland, California. The civil unrest during the 1960s had a heavy impact on my upbringing. I had no choice really. Everywhere I turned, injustice was in my face. It was a time where Blacks started to fight back. We were just so tired of all the hate. We as a people endured that same hate for over 400 hundred years.

Before I went to prison, I was a member of the Black Panther Party for Self Defense. I worked on the newspaper and helped in circumventing anything detrimental to the branch and the organization as a whole.

We were well hated by the police. That's why the organization began in the first place. All the brutality and violence Black people endured in Oakland was crazy. We had no choice, but to organize and stop the violence.

I am one of 8 children and the first of my family to be born in California. My family migrated to California from Athens, Georgia in 1945. We thought we were escaping the cruel south and its brutality. We were wrong. The weather was better, but that's about it. They didn't have mobs to lynch you because they didn't have to.The racist police handled that just fine.

I remember February 2, 1969 like it was yesterday.

✳ ✳ ✳ ✳ ✳

"Ok so our next stop is headquarters right brotha?," I asked Brotha Washington.

"That's right," he said. "We need to meet up and talk about what we're gonna do about these pigs. You know they just killed anotha brotha last night?"

Sam Cooke's A Change Is Gonna Come began to play on the radio.

"This song is so true man," I said.

Just as I said that, a police car pulled up behind us.

"Ok let's just calm down," I said. "We know our rights, we didn't do anything. Just stay under the speed limit."

"Damn they got the lights on us," he said as he pulled to the side of Bancroft Blvd. and 98th Ave. "Is there a problem officer?"

"I'll tell you when there's a problem, don't question me boy," the pig said. "Get outta the car!"

"We haven't done anything thing wrong, we know our rights!" I said.

"Let's go for a walk nigger."

"No, we haven't violated any law."

He grabbed me and threw me on the ground. They beat me in the head with their billy clubs and kicked me in my stomach. I passed out. The next thing I remember is waking up in jail.

My people protested night and day for me to get out. This was headline news. I was being framed for murder. But my lawyer was a complete idiot. So I had to represent myself. I asked God for help, strength and courage.

The trial went on for it felt like an eternity. The prosecution tried to use every trick in the book. Using false witnesses to assassinate my character and the Party, a fake gun. It was just outrageous.

I fought back as best as I could stating that I was knocked unconscious, therefore there was no way I killed anyone.

"We the jurors find Mr. Paul Jackson

guilty for murder in the 1st degree of Oakland Police Officer Joseph Miller."

I felt like I died and officially went to hell. But I refused to give up because I knew I was innocent. I knew that this was the ultimate test and I had to fight back. Otherwise the system was going to win.

"For the heinous act of the murder of Oakland Police Officer Joseph Miller, you are sentenced to life without the possibility of parole," The judge said in a evil tone.

❋ ❋ ❋ ❋ ❋

And the next thing I knew, I was on a bus in handcuffs off to San Quinton for the rest of my life. I don't even know how this happened. I didn't do anything wrong. I'm innocent. All I was trying to do was help defend my people against this racist society. Did I deserve to do life in prison behind that?

I continued to fight for my freedom. And I won't give up. They may have my body, but they will never have my soul. But even though I continued to fight in the court system, I found inner peace because I transcended space and time. I know that I was put in this prison for God's divine plan.

Chapter 4

GETTING TO KNOW MR. CHRISTIANSON

WELL A LITTLE ABOUT ME. My name is Michael James Christianson the third and I am from Walnut Creek, California. My household as a child consisted of my mother and father Michael and Betty Christianson, along with my younger sister Lily. We are from a French, Native American and Black background. You could call us your typical upper middle class family. Nothing out of the ordinary.

My father worked as a doctor and my mother was an excellent stay at home mom. As a Black family we were doing pretty darn good.

I never really had too much of a connection with other Black people. They're just too darn ghetto for me. I was just never exposed to such debauchery. We were blessed to have the finer things in life.

I was always a straight A student and was accepted to Stanford University. After college, I was accepted to U. C. Berkeley's School of Law and studied Corporate Law. I was really good. I made partner at McDonald & Brown, a top law firm in San Francisco, in less than 3 years. But somehow everything just got out of hand. I was soon headline news:

* * * * *

Christianson pleads guilty to embezzlement

San Francisco, CA - Michael Christianson was sentenced to four years and three months in federal prison for embezzling from his former law firm.

Christianson, 36, of Walnut Creek, had pleaded guilty June 2 to wire fraud and money laundering related charges of stealing $10.6 million.

He admitted that he accepted payments from clients without paying his former law firm, McDonald, Brown & Christianson.

* * * * *

I certainly never beyond my wildest nightmares ever fathomed to be imprisoned. I was living so high on the hog, I never thought about how hard I'd fall. First I lost all of my material possessions and when the money ran out, my wife did too.

My first couple of months in prison were so, so heinous. I thought I was going to die in here. But then Elder Jackson took me under his wing and protected me on the condition that I study, pray and meditate. It seems like people shut up when he talked and got out of the way when he walked by. His presence was respected.

I know now that I should have focused my law career on my people. I know it's too late for me, but it's not too late for my best cousin James Christianson. He's coming to visit soon and I'm going to tell him my plan. He's been with me on my journey to enlightenment and I know that he'll use his law degree for good unlike what I did.

"Hey I know that you said that you had something important to tell me?," James asked me through the glass, phone in hand.

"Well, I've given this a lot of thought and I know that you've been with me every step of the way on this journey of learning our real history and just being socially conscious altogether," I said and then took a deep breath. "I have a plan. I always thought you were crazy when you said that you wanted to practice Civil Rights Law, but I get it now. We need to sue America."

"Sue America!?"

"Yes for the atrocities the government

has done to our people. We have more than enough evidence. We have history as proof. We have never received so much as an apology for slavery and for what we endured after slavery all the way up until now. Without slavery America wouldn't even be here."

"Wow."

"Now I know the country is broke, so we will demand an island, wiping our debts clean and paying no taxes. We can use the Native Americans as examples."

"But how would we prove that our ancestors were enslaved? You know that everyone will come out of the wood works and jump on the band wagon."

"We'll use DNA. Trust me, it can be proven. Just because it's difficult doesn't mean it shouldn't be done. It means that we have to do it even more so."

"We're going to need a team of lawyers on this," he said as he looked into space.

"Get your buddies on it, whatever you have to do. This must be done."

"I'm on it."

"Also, in order for our people to truly be ready for real freedom, we need to also start a non profit organization that will be the ultimate learning and training center to help recondition and reeducate their minds. Here is the business plan. Find investors."

"Alright, will do."

Chapter 5

BACK FOR THE 1ST TIME

"Donte' we're going to begin meditation again," Elder Jackson said to me. "This time I want you to sit here in a comfortable position on the floor."

"Aight."

"Cross your legs and put your hands on your knees. Close your eyes and breathe in deeply. Make sure your diaphragm expands as you breathe in. Breathe out slowly. In and out... In and out..."

Sittin here with my eyes closed, I see a world before slavery. A time where our ancestors thrived together in peace. It's hot and sunny. The men and women wear their hair locked and are dressed light for the sun's intense heat. Their dark skin and gold glisten in the sunlight. The market is busy with people selling their goods. The homes are built with great detail. There are pyramids and huge statues of men and women everywhere. I see priests and mothers. I can hear the language of the people and the hustle and bustle of the ancient city.

Everyone there is using the gifts God gave them and are living the righteous path. I began to open my eyes.

"Oh... My... God!" I screamed. I'm free! I'm not in the cell! Am I goin crazy? Oh my God I can't breathe. Wait. I'm getting dizzy.

I woke up to a sweet aroma mixed with the cleanest air I've ever breathed. The sun awakened every nook and cranny of space. How? Am I really in paradise? Let me ask this dude. "Ay, ay man can you tell me where I am?"

"Smbt Kdhp Ldft?" he asked.

"What?"

"Mshd klm?"

"I cain't believe this! I started to walk around, and then I saw it in the distance. So huge, so tall, so new. The Step Pyramid. I'm in Ancient Egypt, I mean Kemet!?! Oh my God! Ok I was meditating IN PRISON and now I'm outside IN KEMET."

The Kemetian stood there looking puzzled trying to understand me.

"I know I look crazy to you. I just cain't believe I'm here. I am Donte'," pointing to my chest and then I pointed to his chest. "What is your name?"

He looked at me for a minute and then said "Mnhtp."

"Umm Umm I, I just can't believe this, I'm in Kemet 4000 years ago. How Did This Happen? Ok, sit down, breathe."

Calm. Down. Think about Elder Jackson in the cell. Breathe using the diaphragm. In and out. In and out.

I slowly opened my eyes.

"Oh shit!" I screamed at the top of my lungs, startling him.

"Are you alright brotha?" Elder Jackson asked soundin shakin and interrupted.

"I-I-I teleported to Egypt uh uh Kemet," I said as I trembled with wide eyes.

"You what?"

"I just went back in time to ancient Kemet," I said barely believing the words as they came out of my mouth. "I channeled being there and when I opened my eyes, I was there. I know it sounds crazy, but watch this time. Gimme those bags over there."

Ok let's see if I can do it again. Close your eyes and think about the inside of a Bank of America vault. Breathe slowly. In and out. In and out. I can feel it this time. I can see it.

"Yes!"

I took as much money as the bags could hold and then I stood perfectly still and closed my eyes and started to think about the cell.

"See!" I said with the bags full of money.

He fainted.

I just stood there for awhile as he slowly came to. When he woke up, I was seated lookin into space.

"Do you know what this means?" Elder Jackson asked in a whisper.

"It's our move," I finally said. A few more minutes passed. "Let's see how far I can go with this. Ok. I want to see if I can get us out."

So we grabbed the bags of money and I took his hands and thought of an island, Cayo Espanto. I saw it in a book. It's green and sunny, filled with all types of fruit trees. I opened my eyes and we were there.

"I just can't believe this," he said trying to catch his breath. Shock was all over his face.

"I'm goin back for the others," I said grinnin from ear to ear.

And one by one I brought the other brothas from our group to the island. And for the rest of the day everybody just celebrated bein free.

"Ok we need a plan," I said to everybody.

"Well what I want to know is exactly what you did to make this happen?" Mike asked. "I want to know if I can do it too."

"Well all we can do is try right?" I asked. "Ok all I did was meditate. I thought about a place I really wanted to be, Kemet."

"But there has to be more to it than just that," Elder Jackson said. "We have been fasting, praying, studying and then meditating. I think you must have ignited the 7 chakras."

"Let's give it a shot," Mike said.

"Ok well let's all sit down in a circle," Elder Jackson said. "Close your eyes, breathe in slowly and think about a place you really want to be. Really try to visualize it. What does it look like? What does it sound like? What does it smell like? Are there people there? What do they look like? Is it hot or cold?

"Alright everyone open your eyes."

"Well that didn't work," Mike said. "Where's Donte?"

It happened again. I was back in Kemet enjoying the sun, the sights and the people. I stayed for a couple of hours this time, just walking around and reflecting on what this all really meant.

I walked down the famous Nile River. The very first cultural highway. It was so beautiful. Fishermen, farmers, mothers, children were all around.

What *does* this all really mean? Why was I the one with this gift? I mean anything I do will change the future forever. I could be selfish and just fix my messed up life, but

71

I know that's not all that God wanted me to do with this. That's not why he gave me this power.

* * * * *

When I got back everyone was asleep, so I left again. I had to clear my head. I had to see her face. See her before she changed.

I remembered going to the park with her when I was a kid. She would push me on the swing and I would go down the slide. We went and had ice cream. She was beautiful.

I see us holding hands walking down the street smiling ear to ear. As I watched us, a single tear ran down my face. I couldn't help it. Damn why?

"Hi," I said to them.

"Oh hi," she replied looking puzzled. "Have we met?"

I had to smile. "Yes. My name is Donte'."

For a few seconds, we just looked into each other's eyes. Her head moved to the side and I could just tell that she saw me, saw her son.

"I just had to see you like this again," as I ran away. I love you ma.

✵ ✵ ✵ ✵ ✵

When I came back to the island, I decided to tell them my plans.

"I got it," I said to the group. "We can go back and right some wrongs. Change the game."

"How exactly?" Mike asked.

"Well for starters I definitely wanna save my panta D's life," I said. "He didn't deserve to go out like that."

"Wait a minute, didn't D get killed right before you came to prison?," Elder Jackson asked with a puzzled look on his face.

"Yeah, wassup?"

"Well think about it, he was alive before you knew you could teleport. If you change that event in history you will have never went to prison and therefore no time travel."

"Exactly, those things in the past had to happen for you to be where you are now," Mike explained.

"Ok well forget that plan," I sighed. We all just thought about it for a minute.

"Well haven't you ever read a story about somebody in history and been like man I wish I coulda helped them?"

"Like who?," Sean asked in a low tone as he thought out loud.

"I don't know. Like save Malcolm X's life or somethin."

"Hmm," Elder Jackson said.

Everybody was quiet for a second.

"Make sure he never gets assassinated?," Sean asked.

"I always wished that somebody was there for him that day. And now we can actually do it. If we fix what happened don't you think today would be so much better?" I asked.

Everybody nodded, rubbed their hands and grinned at each other.

Chapter 6

SAVING MALCOLM

Since we made the decision on when,
everything else was pretty much easy. We
really planned it out. We got more money,
more guns like corner shot launchers, and
double 07 gadgets like MTM special ops
rambo watches, a military UMPC with
GPS and gas masks.

We practiced Japanese and Brazilian Jiu

Jitsu like Cross Grip Sumi Gaeshi, Cross Grip Sumi To The Knee Picks, Defending The Single And Double Leg Takedowns, Breaking Grips, Throw Defenses, Knee Osoto Gari and Hopping Ouchi Gari, for hours each day and weeks on end.

We also studied the location of the murder and figured how to make it not happen.

"Ok so Malcolm was killed February 21, 1965 in Manhattan's Audobon Ballroom," Elder Jackson said to us. "A smoke bomb was thrown up to create a diversion then a man yelled, 'Nigga! Get yo hand outta my pocket!' A man rushed up and shot Malcolm in the chest with a sawed off shotgun and then two other men ran up and shot him 16 more times with handguns."

"These are the pictures of the men," Mike said as he passed out the photos.

"So what we need to do is sit next to the men and get them before they can do this," I said. "So Mike you are going to be on Wilbur McKinley who shouted and threw a smoke bomb, I'll be on William Bradley who had the shotgun and Sean and James will have Leon David and Talmadge Hayer who had the pistols. The rest of you will spread out and guard us just in case."

"Sounds like a plan," Sean said. "Let's get ready."

It wasn't hard finding the killers at all. They looked so obvious as a matter of fact. They were constantly looking left to right and had faces of hate and doubt mixed into one.

Sitting next to William Bradley, I could see that he was so nervous because his leg was twitchin and he was sweatin. I just cain't believe this is the nigga who kills our great leader. I just wanna kill this nigga right now. I was gettin so irritated.

"Let's do it now," I whispered into the ear piece.

"No we gotta wait," Elder Jackson said. "We gotta do this right."

"Alright," I said as I took a deep breath.

And then it was time.

"Nigga get yo hands outta my pocket," Wilbur Kinley yelled.

But there was no smoke bomb this time. Staring at William Bradley I could see that he was totally confused, like he didn't know what to do. But I saw him stand up anyway and before he could reach for his shotgun, my magnum was at his skull.

"Don't even fuckin think about it Willy," I said to him.

He looked startled and confused that I knew his name.

"It's over," I said as I snatched the shotgun from him. "Put yo hands up and start walkin."

People screamed hysterically when they saw what was goin on.

"Everybody just calm down," Elder Jackson said. "We are saving Malcolm X's life today. These men are here to kill him."

As soon as he said that, Malcolm's security team ran over and grabbed the men out of the hall.

Malcolm was able to finish his speech. History was changed forever. When the speech was over and everyone began to walk out, Malcolm and his security motioned us to come over.

"How did you know?" Malcolm asked.

"You wouldn't believe us if we told you," I said. "All I can say is that you must live every second as if it's your last one because today was supposed to be the end. But you are so important to us and to the world as a whole that we couldn't let that happen. We need you."

"Thank you my brothas," he said. "I will take heed to your warning. I already knew my days were numbered. And I truly understand what I have to accomplish before it's all over."

As we walked out I wondered what

exactly was going to happen next. We did it. We actually saved him.

"Ok let's go to the future and see what the impact is," Elder Jackson said.

We went back to the future and nothing changed. There was still crime, murder and chaos all over the world.

"What happened to Malcolm?," I asked.

"Oh my God," Mike gasped. "He was still assassinated," he read slowly. "He was found poisoned September 9, 1969 at a hotel in Harlem. No one was ever apprehended."

"I can't believe this," Elder Jackson said as he scratched his head and walked back and forth.

"Maybe we're not going back far enough," I said. Everyone stood still for a moment.

"You know that I always wanted to help Nat Turner, that story always bothered me. I know that things would have been different if he had some help."

"Yeah maybe the reconstruction period would be different if he had some help," Elder Jackson said.

"The slave rebellion happened August 21, 1831," Mike said.

"So what's the move?" I asked. "Save em and take em back to Africa?"

"That's exactly what we would have to do if we save them," Elder Jackson said. "There's no way they would make it in America."

Chapter 7

NAT

It is summer, the year is 1831 in rural Virginia. Slavery is in full effect. Blacks are deemed 1/10th of a human being and are seen inferior to Whites. They are "owned" and have no control of themselves or their loved ones.

They are forced to work in the fields day in and day out without pay. They are forced to take care of their owners households with sex, cleaning, cooking and tending to every need of anyone the owner demands. Beatings, rape, public humiliation and death are not only common occurrences, but are deemed the norm.

Slave rebellions were the norm as well. And no one was safe. But they always ended the same devastating way, death and more depression.

November 11, 1831 was the day the captors killed Nat Turner. He was murdered for fighting back against being enslaved. We knew we couldn't let that happen again. So we decided that a sneak attack would be the right move.

"We're going back to October 30th 1831,

the day he was captured," I said to the team. "So everybody huddle up." I closed my eyes and took a deep breath. "Here we go."

We found Nat just as we studied, in the hole covered with fence rails.

"You don't have to hide anymore Nat we're here to save you," Elder Jackson said as we pulled him out.

"Y'all sent from God!," he said wide eyed.

"Where is everybody else?" I asked.

He pointed to the right of us.

"Ok everybody spread out and be ready," I whispered.

I slowly started walking with my shotgun in position. I knew they were coming. It was only a matter of time. And sure enough I saw them. That's when I blacked out.

"This is for my ancestors!," I screamed as I shot one in the chest. He didn't stand a chance. "This is for the rape!" I got another one who tried to sneak from around the tree. "You think you're sneaky?," I screamed in hysterics. I kept shooting until I had to reload.

" We should get out of here," Sean yelled as he was shooting his AK-47. "It's looks like it's clear."

"Yeah let's do that," I said trying to snap out of it. "Get everybody together."

"Ok."

I really needed to calm down if I was gonna get us of here. I've never been this worked up in my life. Just breathe. As we all began to hold hands, I started to worry.

"Ok we're going to Africa. Here we go."

I didn't feel any energy this time. We went nowhere. Nothing happened.

"What's wrong?" Mike asked looking anxious.

"I don't know."

"Try again," Elder Jackson said reassuringly.

"Ok." Focus even harder and really dig deep. Breathe. Concentrate. Africa. Bunce Island. Focus.

"Don't tell me we're trapped here Te'," Mike said desperately.

"I think I'm still shaken up," I said. "I need to cool off and try again in a bit. Nat do you think you can take us to a place we can hide?"

"I wreckon I can do that," he said. "Y'all follow me."

This gave us a chance to really see what it was like for our people back then. Really witness the horror, feel the despair. Nat took us to a white family who hid slaves trying to get free. We went into hiding as I tried to calm down and find my center again.

✳ ✳ ✳ ✳ ✳

"Ok so what's the plan?" Mike asked anxiously.

"We need to lay low until I figure out what's wrong with me," I said.

"I understand that, but do we have any

idea what we're really doing?" he said. "We're gonna go back to Africa and then what? Kill all the slave captors and those who were helping them? We don't have enough ammo for that. We'll be shooting forever. This just doesn't look like this will ever be enough. We need to do more... Go further back."

"What do you mean?," I asked.

"Well it seems like we're not making enough of an impact. Saving a few people just isn't enough. We have to realize that this entire country was built on our ancestors backs."

"I know what I gotta do," I said. "I can change it all. I could even make sure this shit never even happened."

"Slavery," Elder Jackson said.

"Exactly."

"Well the Africans traded their enemies to the Arabians 700 hundred years before the Europeans," Mike said.

"We need to make sure we unite the tribes of Africa that were warring with each other," I said. "We gotta do it. I mean we saw what happens if we change just one thing. We gotta get to the core of this man."

"Then we go back to the year 550 A. D.," Mike said.

Everybody thought about it for a while.

"But I think we really gotta talk to our fallen leaders of Kemet," I said. "I think they need to hear what we gotta say."

"Egypt?" Sean asked.

"Kemet is the original name," Elder

Jackson said. "And Imhotep would be an excellent person to inform of this long lasting turmoil the world has had for many millennia. Plus we need to really know what happened back then anyway. Maybe if we help them stay on the path of righteousness and not waver this time it will get us the result we're really looking for."

"Well Imhotep served in the Third Dynasty under Netjerikhet which was around 2650 BC," Sean said. "He was chancellor, high priest, the first engineer, architect and physician. He was even deified as a god. I know he would listen to us."

Chapter 8

KEMET

THE YEAR 2601 BC. THE Step Pyramid at Saqqara in Egypt is practically complete and stands at 200 feet tall. The sunkissed limestone gives the pyramid a holy glow. The complex covers nearly 40 acres and is immaculate, filled with 3 Courts, a Northern and Southern temple, and a House of the North and South.

In Memphis, the capital of Kemet lies a people filled with concentration and purpose. Their tall stature could not be denied. Skin, the color of a deep brass and their hair the texture of wool completed their dominating look. They walked firm and determined because they knew their work would help them enter the afterlife.

"Ok does everyone have their phonetic translators ready?" Mike asked. "We're looking for Imhotep and Netjerikhet."

We walked around for awhile just checkin out the scene. And I must say that was the most magnificent site ever. They worked together to leave a legacy that people would be in awe of thousands of years to come.

A single tear went down my face.

"We gotta keep it like this man," I said. "This is so beautiful. We have to help them stay focused to change the future"

"That's why we're here," Elder Jackson said as we looked around.

A guard walked up to us.

"Greetings we are 4,000 years from the future," Elder Jackson spoke into the translator. "We are here to warn you of the horrible atrocities that will plaque the earth years to come. We are here to tell you that what you do now will impact the future. We must talk to Netjerikhet and Imhotep ."

The guard stood there dumbfounded. "Follow me," he said.

When we found them, they were seated and talking over ancient scrolls.

We informed them of the atrocities that were to come.

"What you must do is unite the people," I said. "This division will only get worse trust me on this," I said to them.

"What he means is that as history continues on, hatred begins to reign as ruler," Mike said. "By the year 1080 BC Kemet falls. Foreign rulers steal the legacy and claim it as their own. History is rewritten. Millions upon millions of people on this continent are persecuted and sold into foreign slavery for hundreds of years to come. A new land is born from the free and forced labor, America. The evil doers never face consequence for their sins. And their descendants continue to wreak havoc on the planet."

"Peace be unto you for coming back and enlightening us to these events in our future which is that of your past," Imhotep said to us with open arms.

"I think I need to show you two," I said as I gestured for us to hold hands.

I took them to Time Square in New York year 2011 AD so that they could really see what we were talking about. We just stood there for a moment and soaked it all in. Imhotep looked around with bewildered eyes, totally shocked and appalled at what he saw. Netjerikhet stood with a sad face.

"If you don't help us, it will be like this," and I pointed to the pollution, a man urinating on the street and a homeless man begging for food and money. We walked around for awhile. At a crosswalk we waited for the ok to cross the street. Once the light turned green we started walking. Suddenly a yellow taxicab came outta no where and almost hit us.

"Watch it you dumb fuck!," the taxicab man yelled at us through the window.

"Are you alright?," I asked as I helped Imhotep up.

"Yes."

We continued to walk and they continued to quietly observe. We came across a hot dog stand. I got them a Coke.

"Here try this."

They stared at it for a long time.

"What is it?," Imhotep asked.

"Poison that we drink everyday. But you have to drink it to understand."

They took a sip and instantly spit it out and started gagging.

"What has happened to us?"

"We don't have a lot of time, but we need your help to fix this." I said.

"Whatever you suggest we will do and when this is done you will be remembered forever," Netjerikhet said.

✱ ✱ ✱ ✱ ✱

When we informed them of the atrocities the future entailed, they kept their word. This gave Kemet a truer purpose, which kept it alive. It started with holding true to the fundamentals of Ma'at, their concept of truth, justice, balance, order, reciprocity and righteousness.

They realized that somehow along the way, Ma'at had been lost. So they cherished it: The prophecy helped them to live righteously.

We united the entire land of Africa... first. We went to Libya.

"We do not come in war," Netjerikhet said to them. "We come in peace."

Then we went to the Sudan and we told the story all over again. We explained to each group what the future would be if they continued to war with one another. Once those lands were united we continued on to Ethiopia and Chad. We continued until the entire continent was in harmony. And then went on to unite the world. Peace, justice, order and righteousness were in full effect throughout the lands. The ancient way of Ma'at was in place.

Since there were no wars, human development advanced to a level never seen before. The ancient secrets of Kemet were never lost. The great mysteries of science, medicine, astrology and architecture were improved every year and progressed past the year that preceded it.

The greatest crime against humanity, the trans-Atlantic slave trade, never happened. Without the free labor, America never happened. The world finally got the chance it never had before to be free of injustice and racism. People got to live in a land without dehumanization. And everyone realized that there is only one race, the human race.

Once the last leader fulfilled his promise,

we began to disappear forever, one by one. So if you're reading this, this is our legacy we pass on to you. Learn from the history. Do not be weak to your lower self. Be better than we ever were. We'll be watching...

Now that I know what is soon to come once the last request has been fulfilled, I feel the need to explain what my world was like and why I decided to make a difference. I want the people of the new future to know what life was like during my time so that they will never give into temptation and to create a new righteous path.

Well there is a lot to be said about the current condition of the planet Earth in the 21st century. The planet is still plagued by the crimes that were committed against humanity centuries prior. Many centuries ago, millions of people of a darker hue were taken from their homeland and forced to perform free labor for over 500 years. This free labor created a new land that originally belonged to the Native Indigenous population but was stolen from them. The captors named the stolen land America. And they never received any consequence for the rape, murder and enslavement of the millions of captives they brought to the stolen land.

Due to the free labor, America became the most powerful nation in the world. The captives were eventually free, but were never considered equal. They were constantly belittled, beaten and murdered because of what was done to them and their ancestors in the past.

But it grew to take its toll. And

America became in debt due to its greed and corrupt actions. It was riddled with crime and poverty. Other countries owned America because of this great and constant accumulating debt. And America began to war with everyone for control.

I was born February 28, 1990 in Oakland, California and born right into the poverty. Everyone had to perform various crimes just to survive. The government that once controlled the slave trade didn't care at all about the descendants of the enslaved who built the country. The institution never apologized or did anything to try and fix the serious and sensitive issue. So the vicious cycle of poverty and desperation continued to plague the inner city communities generation to generation.

Other nationalities would move in amongst the crazy atmosphere, adding another dynamic that would cover the real issue of injustice and discrimination. Some would make it out of the poverty, but because they were so embarrassed and ashamed to ever have been poor, they would deny they were ever there. They would turn their back on the very community that embraced them and never shunned them out, while running to the establishment that always did the opposite.

These are the reasons why I chose to take a stand. When I found that I had the power, I did what I felt in my heart was right. And I know that is why God gave me the gift. To fix the wrongs and start over.

Chapter 9

THE AFTERMATH

IT IS THE YEAR 4511. Earth is a wonderful, serene and harmonious place. Studying our history revealed a time when that was not always so. We read of horrific wars and famines. And how time was changed forever by a great man who had the ability to time travel. The great Donte' Jones left behind the scrolls of how it happened so that we would never forget. So that we could see how low we could go and to never let our lower selves prevail in that way again.

And because of this brave heroic act, Earth grew stronger. We came together for the betterment of humanity and nature. Society was and is truly righteous. We know that is the ultimate reward.

As a result, we've learned to mind travel for some time now. It is an art of using the eastern and western hemispheres of your brain to visualize where you want to be. To be on this level, one must meditate and study. It is a treasured skill that shows where you are spiritually. You cannot mind travel without peace and humility. It is impossible. The brain does not allow it, which is truly a blessing. It makes balance in our society. If you want great gifts, you must live purely.

We have great universities with a foundation our ancestors have used for thousands of years, ma'at: truth, justice, righteousness, balance, order, reciprocity. We know we are not perfect, but we must always strive for perfection. We study new ways to advance ourselves to the next level of development. We know that it is our divine plan.

We do not bother ourselves with monetary gain because that is not the path to enlightenment. Each person uses their special talents for the betterment of the everyone. Our land has prospered so much from this. We were shown how devastated the planet would be if we succumbed to greed and hate.

In doing so, we have been able to communicate with life forms across our great galaxy and beyond using telepathy.

We have all agreed on peace. To come and go as we please with no violence.

I am Manu Hovmey of the planet Earth. I am married to a wonderful woman, Canwe', and we have two beautiful children, Manu II and Olape.

I am an engineer for the National Galactic Council. We are currently building a highway that will connect our galaxy once and for all. We are currently partnering with neighboring planets to get this show on the road, literally. We've been working on this project for about forever. But every life form has their own time schedule, so what can you do? Currently the planet's Opptu, Frejk and Sidveb have responded but we're still waiting on Kiqjuof and Gercesd to give their feedback, otherwise we will have to decide for them. I don't understand why it's so difficult to respond in a timely manner.

Anyway, I just got back from this romantic galactic cruise with me and my wife. It was a fantastic 8 week trip to 2 galaxies: Jepui and Kahlo. Everyday was a different planet. We explored the shores of planet Iru where it never gets dark and is always sunny. I loved it, but to be honest I was ready to go by the end of *my* day. I mean when do you go to sleep? The Irunians were actually really nice though. They really knew how to party. Don't go there if you can't hang.

Too many stories to tell. Let's see there was the planet Pfedcu in Kahlo. Now the reason I mention them is because this planet is somewhere I just might move to because it was so, uh, what's the word I'm looking for, uh, mellow. Very calm, I love that. Not boring because there were plenty of activities, but no human judgment that

Earth has. No stupid flaws like jealousy or sadness. I mean Earth is pretty darn close. Ma'at has helped us keep balance, but Pfedcucians certainly have charisma. They look like they don't try at all. It's just who they are. We on the other hand have to work at it night and day.

On the way back, I began to think about why it's so hard for us to be good naturally. I mean if it weren't for Donte Jones going in back in time and informing our ancestors of the future, who knows where we'd be. I mean I know it's our genetic makeup and all, but I guess when I saw the Pfedcucians who were all perfect and not even trying, I realized how much harder we have it. We still have a long way to go before we ever get there.

All I know is when I got back I was completed exhausted. I really missed home. Nothing like it. We work hard and play hard. I love the balance in that. And our planet loves us back for it. When we finally got the whole human violence thing under control, she actually began to talk to us. And our relationship couldn't be better. We finally realized that we needed to stop killing her in order to save ourselves. So we created things that made our lives easier and not destroy her at the same time.

We even communicate with the animals now. And from what I studied, it didn't used to be that way. Before we would actually *eat* them. It really wasn't that difficult. They were already trying to talk to us, we just weren't listening.

✳ ✳ ✳ ✳ ✳

"Any feedback from planets Kiqjuof and

Gercesd," I asked Jana who also helped with the Council.

"No we still haven't heard anything from them yet," she said. "We've uh actually gotten word that they've vanished. And an unknown planet has appeared in the center of the vacant space."

"What?"

"Yes, well reports keep coming in of a different planet altogether. And the other planets are just gone. No one can explain it," she said frantically.

"Get Dr. Cuani on it," I whispered.

Not there? A new planet? This makes absolutely no sense at all. How could this be? Vanished? Who would do this?

"Get Phaj Utima on the line," I said.

Maybe he knows what's going on.

"Why didn't you tell me about this?," I asked.

"You were on vacation," Phaj exclaimed. "We thought we'd have the glitch figured out, but we discovered that it's not a glitch. This is real."

"Real, what could do this?" I demanded. "We don't live by these laws. I know it wasn't an accident."

"No it definitely wasn't an accident," he said slowly. "Um we actually think that we've known this would happen for some time. The ancients always talked about the possibility of significant impact Donte' Jones had on our universe."

"Impact?"

"Yes, well just think about, the great

Donte' Jones had the ability to teleport through time and he decided to change past events to impact the future. Once the last event was changed, an alternate universe began. But whatever happened to the other universe? Where did it go?"

"Ok we're here today because we have some issues that we need to figure out and you are the only ones who can help us," I said to the group of elders.

"So what is going on?," Elder Hajmon asked.

"Well it seems that planets Kiqjuof and Gercesd have mysteriously disappeared and a new planet has appeared in their place," I said.

"Just like the prophecy of Gynsapa said," Priest Monsal said. "The other universe is fighting to come back."

"Come back?" I asked.

"Yes when the history was altered, the universe disappeared," Hajmon said. "Their universe's forces are fighting to reappear."

"But what do we do?" I asked.

"The ALL," they said in unison.

"The ALL is summoned by uniting the energy of our entire universe." Monsal said.

"How do we do that?" I asked.

"Well in essence, we must use meditation to connect our minds to the core of every planet and those planets must unite together to combat the force that is trying to come back," Monsal said.

"Sounds easy enough."

"Not quite," Hajmon said. "In order to connect every mind, we must be in perfect harmony. This will truly test where we are as a whole. Otherwise it simply won't be enough positive energy."

"Well the majority of us are able to mind travel, so that's definitely a good indicator of where we are, we can do this," I said.

"But now we have to help those who cannot mind travel because they refused to live the righteous path," Monsal said.

"How much time do we have?" I asked Phaj.

"Well looking at how quickly Kiqjuof and Gercesd disappeared, we definitely don't have much time at all. I'd say about a month tops before our entire galaxy is gone," he said smugly.

"Well we gotta get to work," I said. "Phaj, inform the other planets of what needs to be done and we must find those who do not mind travel with a mass conference."

* * * * *

Tired of traveling the long way? Don't know how to mind travel and want to learn quickly? Connect with to us, we're the experts. Learn to bridge the western and eastern hemispheres of your brain in a snap. It's as easy as 1-2-3! Mass Mind Traveling Seminar 24/7! Connect now! Refer a friend and get a free gift!

"Ok we're going to begin this digital seminar for Mind Traveling," I said. "We will begin the process first with deep meditation either lying on the floor or in a reclining chair. Take slow, deep breaths to relax your mind and body.

"As you begin, relax and visualize another room in your home as clearly and with much detail as possible. If you can't think visually, then try to use your other senses like noises.

✳ ✳ ✳ ✳ ✳

"So how did we do on the numbers?," I asked Jana.

"We did very well actually, we had roughly 90 million converters," she said excitedly.

"But that's still not enough." I sighed. "There are 10 billion inhabitants and only

2 billion can mind travel. We have a long way to go. Do we have enough time? Get me Elder Hajmon."

✻ ✻ ✻ ✻ ✻

"What are we going to do?" I whispered.

"This is the battle of universes and the lost souls. One will win. And it has to be the righteous who will be victorious in the end."

"But why now?" I asked. "Why not thousands of years ago?"

"I think that he first realized he had the gift of time travel around this year," he said. "I believe they called it 2011 A. D."

"We can't just sit here and vanish!"

"Maybe we can live in together in

harmony. I mean 2 planets disappeared and 1 appeared," he slowly said.

"Harmony?," I asked. "But how?"

"I'm not sure, but this may be the end of the world as we know it to be."

"Well, the first thing we need to do is go to this new planet," I said hesitantly.

TO BE CONTINUED...

Urban Dictionary

1. Blood - Friend

2. Bruh - Friend / Brother

3. Bucket - Old car

4. Conasto - Corner store

5. Cuzzo - Friend / Cousin

6. Cut - To leave

7. Dipped out - To have left in a haste

8. Feelins - Feelings

9. Fien - Short for Dope Fiend or someone who is addicted to crack cocaine or heroin

10. Finna - About to

11. Gone - Going to

12. Grapes - A high quality marijuana that is formed into dark purple buds resembling grapes

13. Gravy - All good

14. Hands - The ability to drive well

15. Hella - Really, a lot of

16. Hen - Hennessy

17. Hit me - Contact me

18. Keep it real - Be honest

19. Murked - Murdered

20. OG - Original Gangster

21. On mommas - On everything

22. One hunnid - One hundred percent, be honest

23. Poppin - Going on

24. Rack - 1 Year or 1 thousand dollars

25. Scraper - Old car

26. Shanked - To be stabbed in prison with a make shift knife

27. Slangin - Selling drugs

28. Smash - To drive very fast

29. Split - To leave

30. Tha Town - Oakland, California

31. Trife life - Despicable, grimy lifestyle

32. Whip - Car

About the Author

Trina Renee', a young African American woman, has learned a lot from the streets of Oakland, California, home of the Black Panther Party, racial injustice and police brutality. She has seen what it takes to make it in the inner city. Against all odds she was determined to fight back and clean up the black community. This is her contribution.